A.D. 66   A.D. 141   A.D. 218   A.D. 295   A.D. 374

A.D. 530   A.D. 607   A.D. 684   A.D. 760   A.D. 837

A.D.   A.D. 912   A.D. 989   A.D. 1066   A.D. 1145   A.D. 1222

Halley Came to Jackson

WRITTEN AND PERFORMED BY

MARY CHAPIN CARPENTER

ILLUSTRATED BY DAN ANDREASEN

HARPERCOLLINS*PUBLISHERS*

For backyard astronomers of all ages, and to Marcie, with thanks

—M.C.C.

To the children of Emma L. Smith Elementary School

—D.A.

Halley Came to Jackson   Text copyright © 1998 by Mary Chapin Carpenter and EMI April Music Inc.   Illustrations copyright © 1998 by Dan Andreasen   Printed in China. All rights reserved.   http://www.harperchildrens.com   "Halley Came to Jackson" was published in 1990 by EMI, April Music, Inc., and Getarealjob Music.   Library of Congress Cataloging-in-Publication Data   Carpenter, Mary Chapin.   Halley came to Jackson / written and performed by Mary Chapin Carpenter ; pictures by Dan Andreasen   p.   cm.   Summary : A father shows his baby daughter Halley's comet as it soars across the Jackson sky in 1910, and as an old woman she returns to her childhood home to see it again in 1986.   ISBN 0-06-025400-9.   [1. Halley's comet—Fiction.   2. Comets—Fiction.   3. Stories in rhyme.]   I. Andreasen, Dan, ill.   II. Title. PZ8.3.C1995Hal 1998 97-34354   [E]—dc21 CIP AC   Typography by Al Cetta   1 2 3 4 5 6 7 8 9 10 ❖   First Edition

Almost ten years ago, a friend suggested I read Eudora Welty's *One Writer's Beginnings*, a collection of Ms. Welty's essays about growing up in Jackson, Mississippi, and the experiences that nurtured her ambition as a young adult to become a writer. Since that first reading, I have returned to the book countless times, for wisdom and inspiration, and for the rewards it offers to anyone who has ever felt the spark of creativity. It was a family story of her father bringing the infant Eudora over to the window to witness the comet Halley's 1910 visit that inspired the song "Halley Came to Jackson." The song thereafter appeared on my 1990 album, *Shooting Straight in the Dark*.

In May of 1996, the first Eudora Welty Film and Fiction Festival took place in Jackson for the purpose of raising funds for the Eudora Welty Writer's Center. The center is located in the very house that is so much a part of Ms. Welty's stories in *One Writer's Beginnings*. I had the privilege of joining other musical performers on an evening in Jackson when tribute was paid to Ms. Welty not only as a great artist, but as a treasured member of the community. When it came my turn to perform "Halley Came to Jackson," I was thick in the throat and wobbly in the knees, nervous yet thrilled by the magical circumstances that allowed me to be a part of the celebration. I will never forget it.

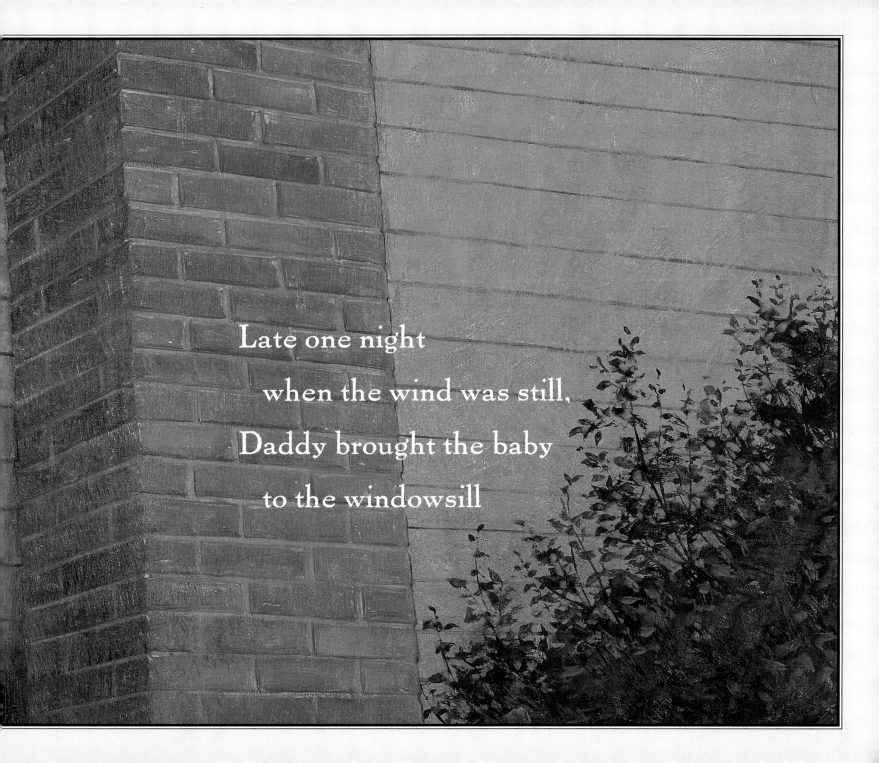

Late one night
when the wind was still,
Daddy brought the baby
to the windowsill

To see a bit of heaven

shoot across the sky,

The one and only time

Daddy saw it fly.

It came from the east
just as bright as a torch.
The neighbors had a party
on their porch.

Daddy rocked the baby,
Mother said amen
When Halley came to visit
in 1910.

Now back then

Jackson was a real small town.

And it's not every night

a comet comes around.

It was almost eighty years
   since its last time through.
So I bet your mother
   would have said amen too.

As its tail stretched out
like a stardust streak,
The papers wrote about it
every day for a week.

You wondered where it's going
and where it's been
When Halley came to Jackson
in 1910.

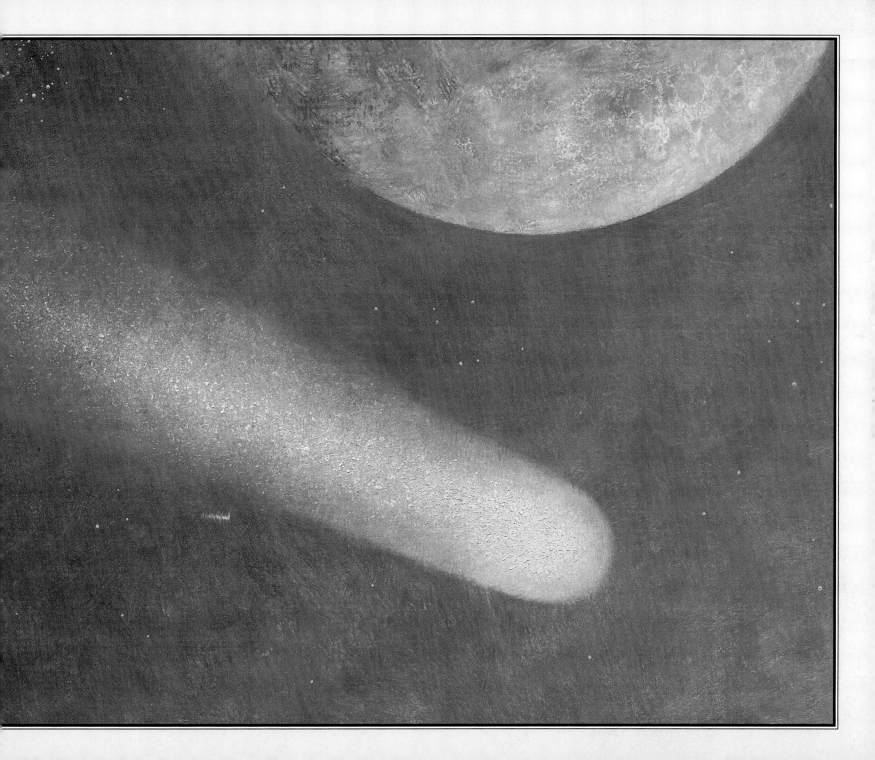

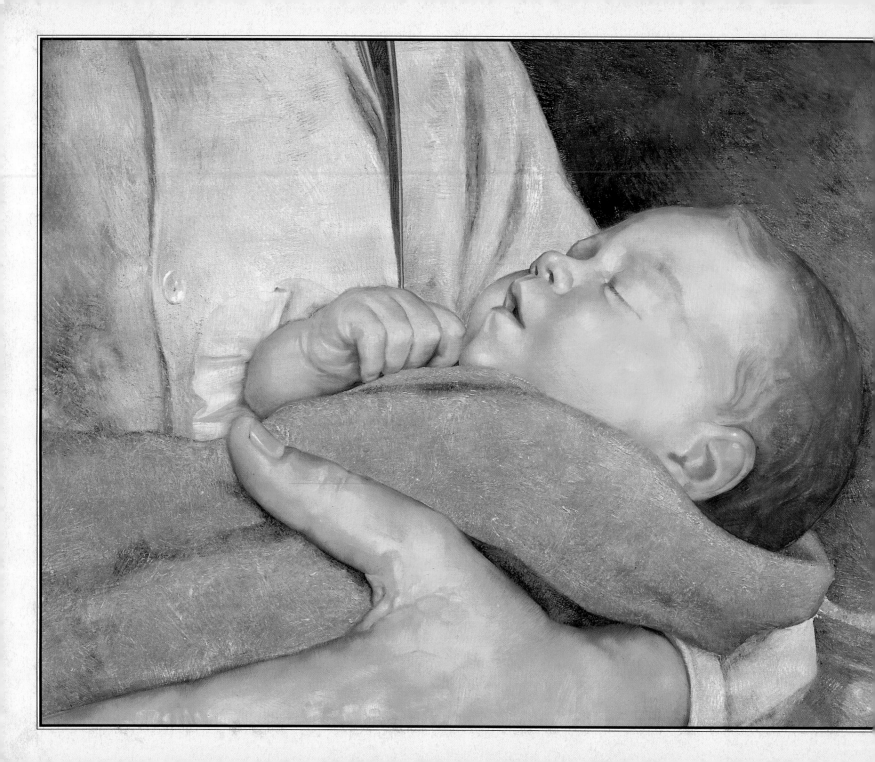

Now Daddy told the baby

sleeping in his arms

To dream a little dream

of a comet's charms.

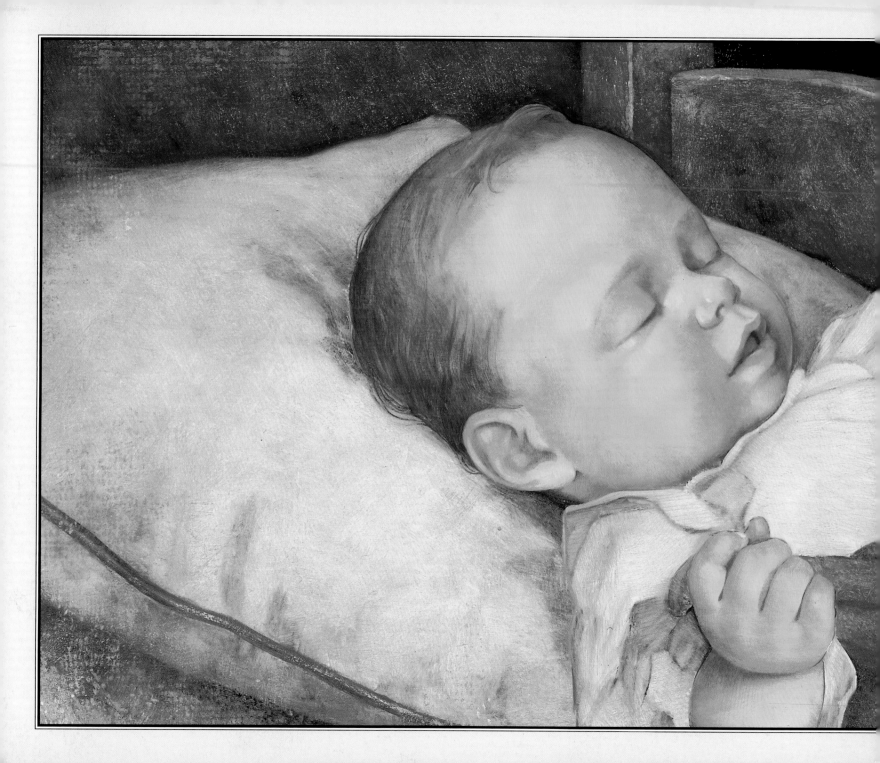

And he made a little wish
as she slept so sound.

In 1986
that wish came 'round.

It came from the east
just as bright as a torch.
She saw it in the sky
from her daddy's porch.

As heavenly sent
as it was back then
When Halley came to Jackson
in 1910.